The Problem with NOT Being Scared of Monsters

Dan Richards

Illustrated by
Robert Neubecker

BOYDS MILLS PRESS
AN IMPRINT OF HIGHLIGHTS
Honesdale, Pennsylvania

For Anna & Paul
 —DR

For Isidore
 —RN

Text copyright © 2014 by Dan Richards
Illustrations copyright © 2014 by Robert Neubecker
All rights reserved
For information about permission to reproduce selections from this book,
contact permissions@highlights.com.

OCT 2 9 2014

Boyds Mills Press
An Imprint of Highlights
815 Church Street
Honesdale, Pennsylvania 18431
Printed in Malaysia

ISBN: 978-1-62091-024-5
Library of Congress Control Number: 2014931590

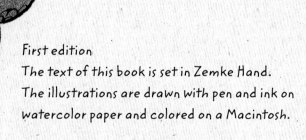

First edition
The text of this book is set in Zemke Hand.
The illustrations are drawn with pen and ink on
watercolor paper and colored on a Macintosh.

10 9 8 7 6 5 4 3 2 1

The problem with **NOT** being scared
of monsters is...

...they think **you're** one of **them**.

It's **hard** to climb out of bed in the morning.

Your breakfast cereal tastes **funny**.

You can't **fini**sh your work.

Things get **carried** away at recess.

Walking home is a **drag**.

Snack takes **f o r e v e r** to clean up.

There's **never** enough hot water.

Your favorite pajamas
are **always** in the wash.

Every little sound
keeps you **awake** at night.

Sometimes all you can do is **hide** and hope no one finds you.

And just when you've had **all** you can take...

...something truly **scary** comes along.

What's that?

There's a M**O**nster under your bed?

No problem.